WHAT NOISE DO I MAKE?

Brian McLachlan

Owlkids Books

For my two sons, who make their own amazing noises.

Owlkids Books acknowledges the financial support of the Canada Council for the Arts, the Ontario Arts Council, the Government of Canada through the Canada Book Fund (CBF) and the Government of Ontario through the Ontario Media Development Corporation's Book Initiative for our publishing activities.

Published in Canada by
Owlkids Books Inc.
10 Lower Spadina Avenue
Toronto, ON M5V 2Z2

Published in the United States by
Owlkids Books Inc.
1700 Fourth Street
Berkeley, CA 94710

Library and Archives Canada Cataloguing in Publication

McLachlan, Brian, author

    What noise do I make? / Brian McLachlan.

ISBN 978-1-77147-150-3 (bound)

    1. Animal sounds--Juvenile literature. I. Title.

QL765.M33 2016   j591.59'4   C2015-907793-1

Library of Congress Control Number: 2015957719

Edited by: John Crossingham and Karen Li
Designed by: Claudia Dávila

Manufactured in Dongguan, China, in June 2016, by Toppan Leefung Packaging & Printing (Dongguan) Co., Ltd.
Job #BAYDC26

A   B   C   D   E   F

hOOt

Publisher of Chirp, chickaDEE and OWL
www.owlkidsbooks.com | Owlkids Books is a division of

cat

dog

snake

alligator

dolphin

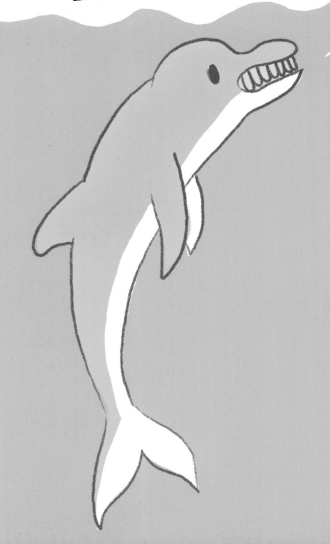

whale

walrus

horse

zebra

hippopotamus

rhinoceros

elephant

giraffe*

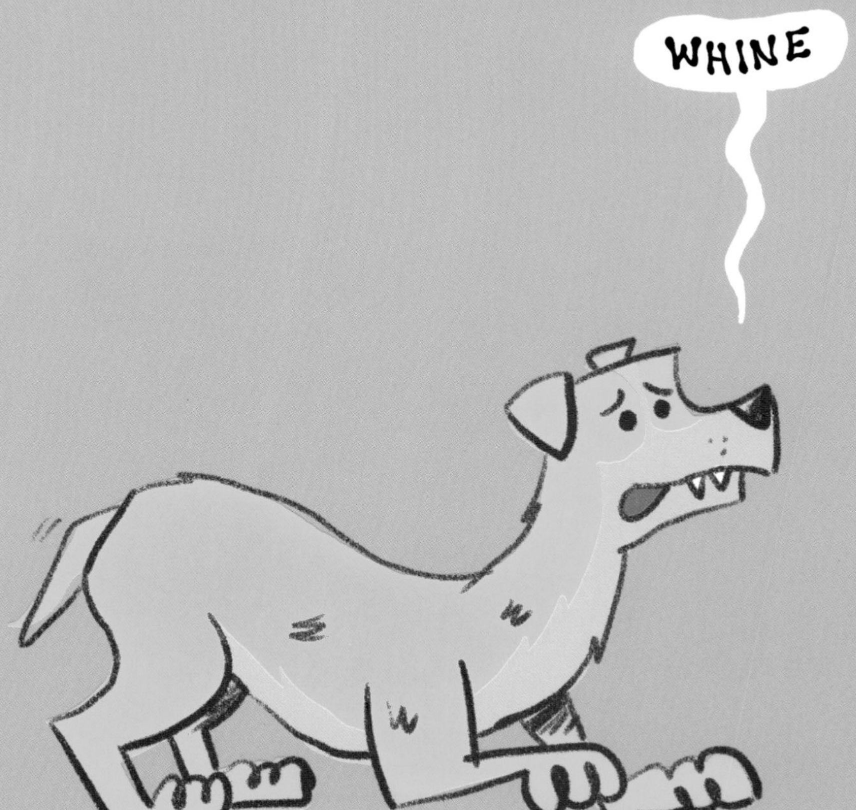
WHINE

penguin

pangolin

ostrich

pelican

swan

flamingo

kookaburra

peacock

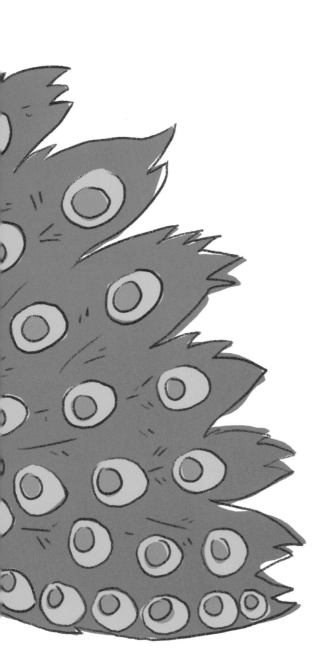

giant panda

red panda

beaver

cicada

bat

aye-aye

tree frog

fox

skunk

raccoon

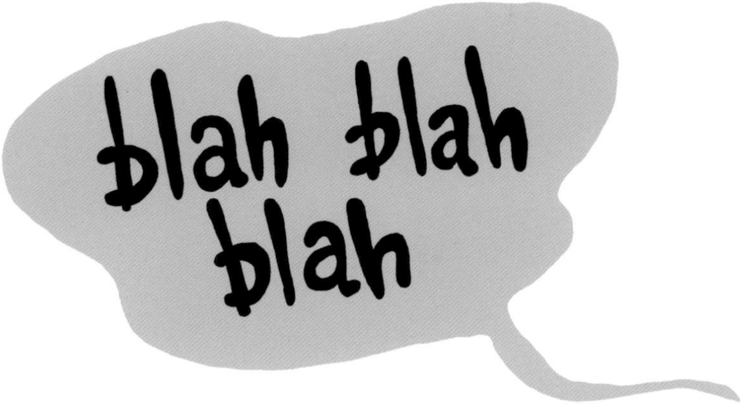
blah blah blah

chimpanzee

orangutan

gibbon

tamarin

*giraffes can talk but usually don't.